Praise for my other books

'Will make you laugh out loud, cringe and snigger, all at the same time'
-LoveReading4Kids

'Very funny and cheeky'
-Booktictac, Guardian Online Review

Waterstones Children's Book Prize Shortlistee!

'I LAUGHED SO MUCH, I THOUGHT THAT I WAS GOING TO BURST!'
Finbar, aged 9

'The review of the eight year old boy in our house...
"Can I keep it to give to a friend?"
Best recommendation you can get' -Observer

'HUGELY ENJOYABLE, SURREAL CHAOS'
-Guardian

I am still not a Loser
WINNER of
The Roald Dahl
FUNNY PRIZE
2013

First published in Great Britain 2015
by Jelly Pie an imprint of Egmont UK Ltd
The Yellow Building, 1 Nicholas Road, London W11 4AN

Bunky is a Loser first published online for *We Love This Book*, 2012

I am Nit a Loser first published for World Book Day 2014

Text and illustration copyright © Jim Smith 2012, 2014, 2015
The moral rights of the author-illustrator have been asserted.

ISBN 978 1 4052 7592 7

barryloser.com
www.jellypiecentral.co.uk
www.egmont.co.uk

A CIP catalogue record for this title is available from the British Library

Printed and bound in Great Britain by the CPI Group

59007/1

Jelly Pie

MIX
Paper
FSC   FSC® C018306

Barry Loser's

ultimate book of Keelness!

Eyes dotted by

Jim Smith

Hello!

Welcome to the keelest Barry Loser book ever! It's sort of a collection of short stories, amazekeel loserfacts, quizzes to find out how much of a loserfan you are and other stuff like that.

— my nose

There's even an extract from the new FUTURE RATBOY book that's SO KEEL there needs to be a new word to say how keel it is.

Future, Ratboy's nose

Contents

Meet the Losers! 8

Design your own Fronkle . . 14

Draw an elephant 16

How to draw a Loser 19

Loserfact 27

Test your loserish memory . . 28

Darren's no nose 30

Spot the difference 31

Dog poos! 32

Loserfact 35

Who Bunky is based on 36

Bunky is a Loser 39

Freaky Feeko's 66

The Daily Poo 69

Design your own paper 74

Not knock jokes 76

Ringpulls! 80

I am NIT a Loser 85

Draw some bugs 220

Loserfact 221

Talk like a Loser 222

My 10 keelest questions ever . . 224

Not Not Bird 236

Guess the nose 238

The loserfan quiz 240

Design a superhero 244

Future Ratboy sneaky peek . . . 246

Meet the Losers!

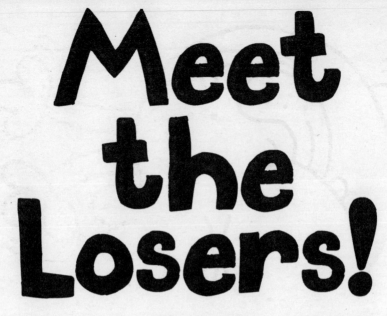

NAME: Barry Loser
KEELNESS LEVEL: V. keel
CATCHPHRASE: 'KEEEEL!'
JOB: Being keeeeeeeeel

colour me in

draw my nose!

NAME: Bunky
KEELNESS LEVEL: High
CATCHPHRASE: 'Salute!'
JOB: Barry's sidekick

9

NAME: Nancy Verkenwerken
KEELNESS LEVEL: Quite keel
CAT'S NAME: Gregor Verkenwerken
JOB: Working stuff out for Barry

NAME: Darren Darrenofski
KEELNESS LEVEL: Medium
FAVOURITE DRINK: Fronkle
JOB: Burping in faces

NAME: Sharonella
KEELNESS LEVEL: Average
FANCIES: Barry Loser
JOB: Being bossy

NAME: Gordon Smugly
KEELNESS LEVEL: Unkeel
CAT'S NAME: Spencer
JOB: Being all smug

NAME: Anton Mildew
KEELNESS LEVEL: Loserish
BEST FRIEND: Invis
JOB: Editor, The Daily Poo

12

NAME: Future Ratboy
KEELNESS LEVEL: KEEL
CATCHPHRASE: 'KEEL!'
JOB: Superduperhero

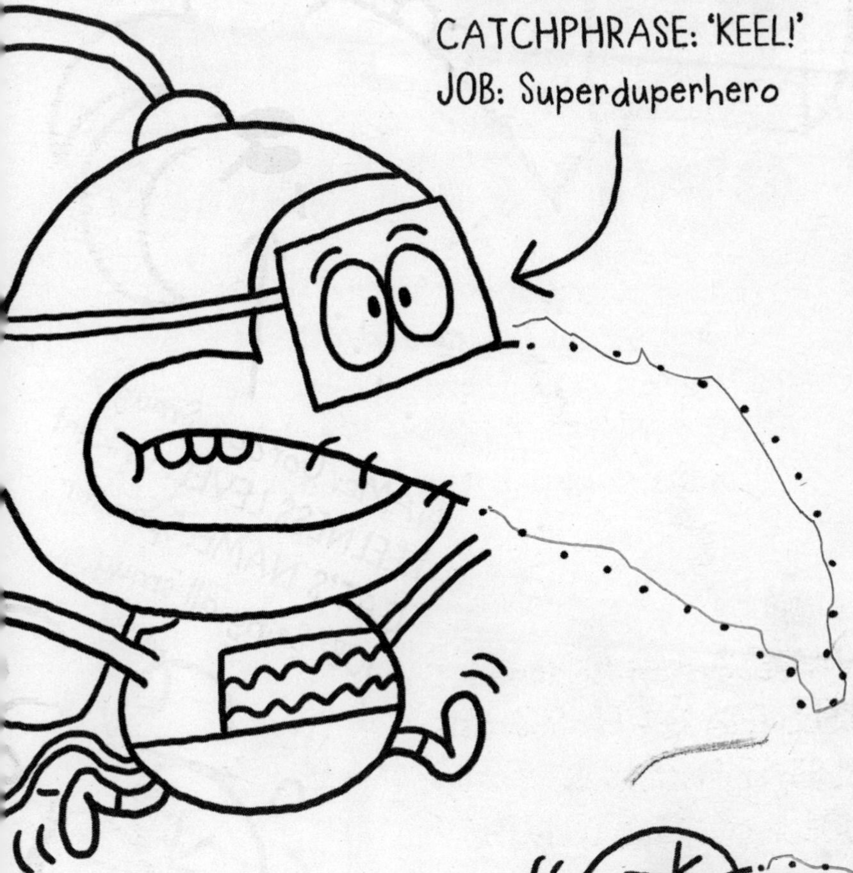

NAME: Not Bird
KEELNESS LEVEL: Kee-heel
CATCHPHRASE: 'NOT!'
JOB: Future Ratboy's sidekick

13

Design your own Fronkle

When my eye dotterer Jim Smith was my age, he had a keeeeel collection of soft drink cans from all over the world. That's why he invented the drink 'Fronkle' and put it in my books.

Draw an elephant

Or don't.

Hold this page
up to the light.

(not really)

How to draw a Loser

Here's what you'll need:

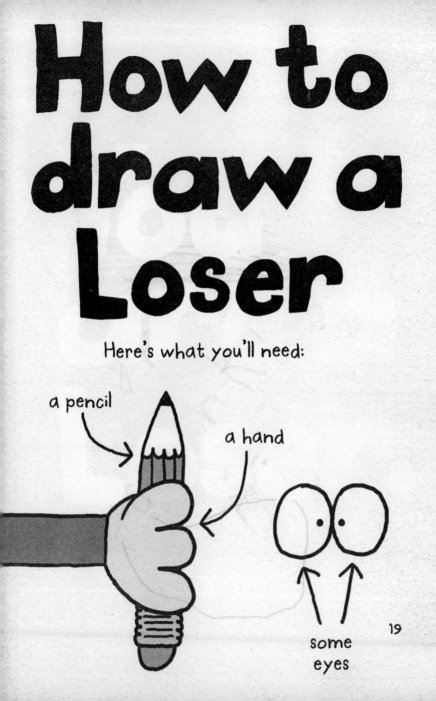

a pencil

a hand

some eyes

19

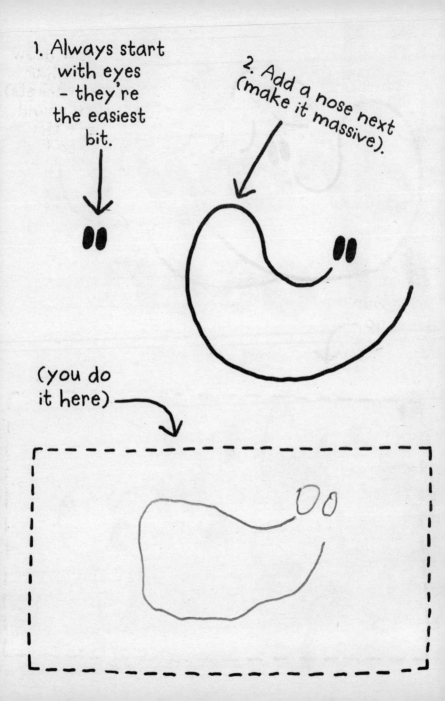

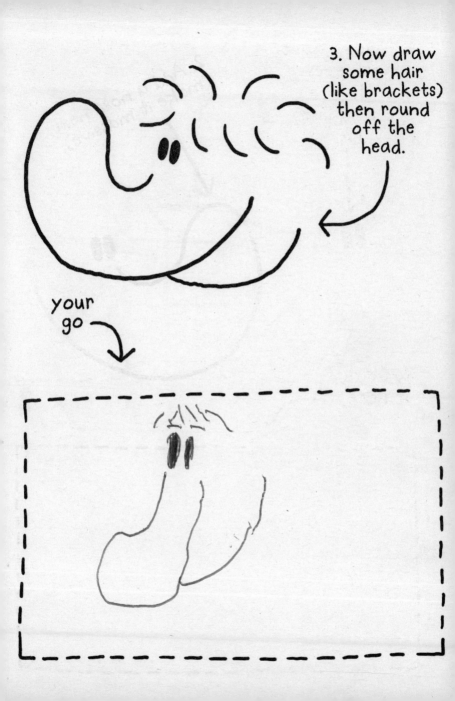

3. Now draw some hair (like brackets) then round off the head.

your go →

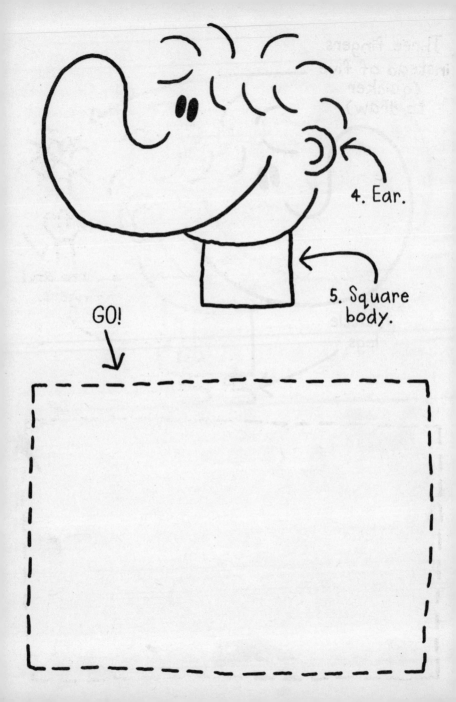

4. Ear.

5. Square body.

GO!

10. Here are some ways to give your characters feelings, just with eyebrows . . .

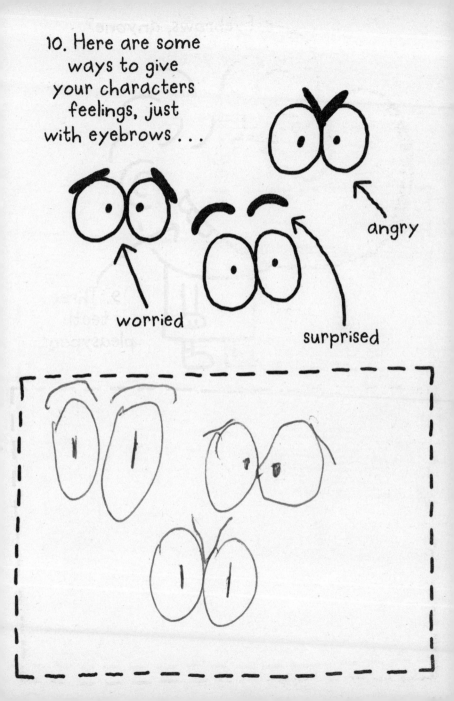

angry

worried

surprised

Now get a mirror
and draw yourself!

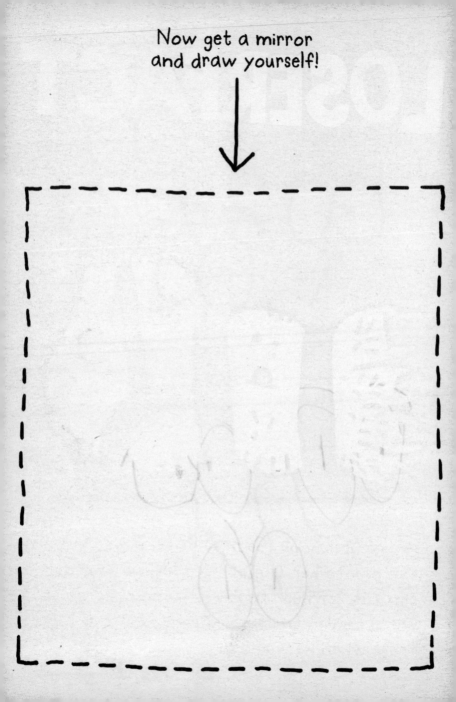

LOSERFACT

In my first book, Granny Harumpadunk bumps into her friend Ethel, whose feet are too fat for her sandals. Ethel's feet are based on Jim Smith's dinner lady's feet from when he was a kid.

Test your loserish memory

In 'I am so over being a Loser' (my yellow book), me and my friends all start collections. Can you remember who collected what?

A. ringpulls

B. jewellery

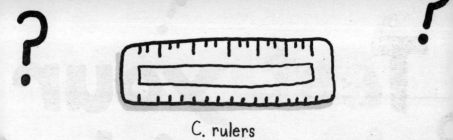

C. rulers

- - - - - - - - - - -

D. sweets

E. boring old tea towels

- - - - -   - - - - -

F. keel napkins

G. stamps

- - - - - - -

- - - - - -

Darren's no nose

Darren Darrenofski's nose has fallen off. Can you remember which one is his? Draw it back quick so he can smell his blowoff!

A

B

C

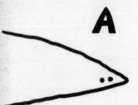

Spot the difference

Can you spot the difference between these two pictures of Not Bird?

Dog poos!

There are lots of dog poos in my books, mostly because dog poos are disgusting and keel. Here are some extra-weird ones for you to enjoy.

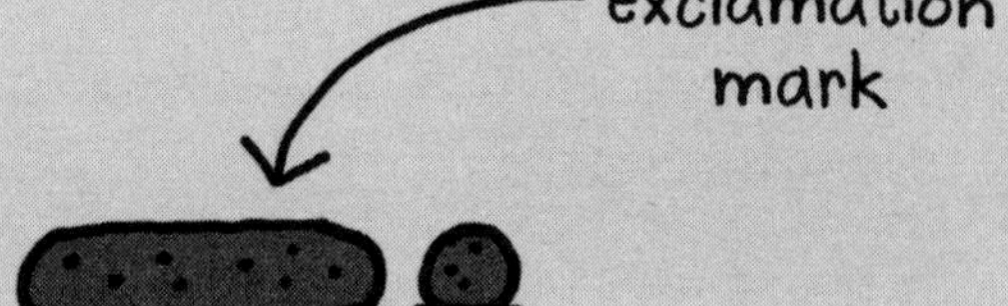

sideways
exclamation
mark

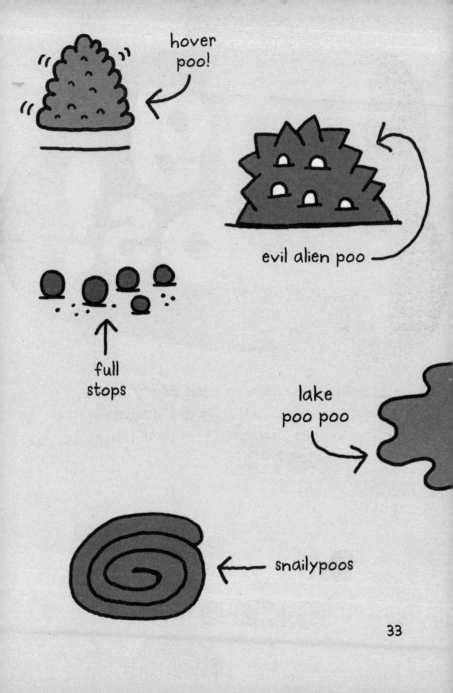

hover poo!

evil alien poo

full stops

lake poo poo

snailypoos

person
stuck
in poo

Now do your own!
(drawing, not poo).

LOSERFACT

You know Mrs Trumpet Face from my blue book, 'I am NOT a Loser'? Well, she was a real person who lived down Jim Smith's road when he was a kid.

She was always shouting at him and his friends like a trumpet. That's why they called her Mrs Trumpet Face.

Who Bunky is based on

My best friend Bunky is based on Jim Smith's best friend when he was a kid.

Bunky

on his way round at 7am

He was called Ben, and he was ALWAYS round Jim's house. During the summer holidays, Ben turned up round Jim's house so early every morning that Jim was usually still in bed.

Not that that bothered
Ben. Jim's mum would let
him in, and he'd make
himself at home,
watching TV and having
a spot of breakfast.

When Jim finally got up
and came downstairs, he'd
get all annoyed to find
Ben sitting on his sofa,
living JIM'S life. So he'd
send him home.

Jim would calm down
after about twenty
minutes and call Ben up,
ordering him to come
back round to play. Which
is sort of how I act with
Bunky in my books.

1980s
phone

37

Talking of Bunky, here's a little story about me getting annoyed with him for being really annoying. Enjoykeels! →

looks like
a little dress

Saturday morning poo

I could tell it was the weekend when I woke up, because my dad had done his extra-smelly Saturday morning poo then tried to cover it up with aftershave and the whole of the upstairs of my house completely stank of poo and aftershave.

secretly quite like it →

I wrapped a pillow round my head and rolled out of bed.

I crawled along the floor to the stairs and got into the pillowcase, then slid down on my bum, doing a blowoff on each bounce.

WHOOSH!

PARP!

BUMP!

When I got to the bottom, my
best friend Bunky was watching
Future Ratboy on TV in the living
room, which didn't surprise me
because he's round my house
more than he's round his.

eating my
cereal

'Poowee, what's that stink?' he said.

'You!' I said, and I spun the chair he
was sitting on, which is one of those
ones you can twizzle round.

The twizzle

'WAAAHHHHHH!!!' screamed Bunky, his cereal flying off in every direction, including my mouth.

The cereal was in the shape of UFOs, so they looked pretty keel as they whizzed through the air and landed on my tongue, and I imagined the little aliens inside being crushed to death as I chomped.

Weirdly, the episode of **Future Ratboy** that was playing on TV had UFOs in it as well, so I said, 'Let's play UFOs!' and we ran up to my room, which still stank a bit, although that is pretty normal.

'Alien attack!' shouted Bunky, throwing a remote control car at my head the millisecond we got into the room.

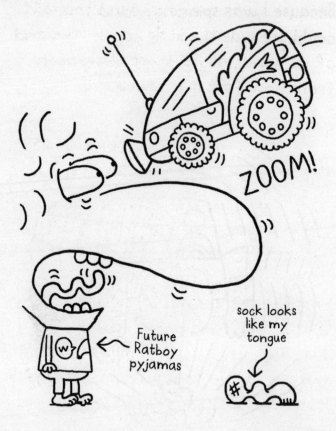

ZOOM!

Future Ratboy pyjamas

sock looks like my tongue

'OWWWW,' I girl-screamed, and I picked up the car by its aerial and started swinging it like a lasso.

Because I was spinning round too, all I could see was the little car on the end of its aerial, all its doors flung open from how fast it was going.

SWOOSH!

'WATCH OUT!' shouted Bunky, as the car slipped out of my hand and flew towards the jar that sits on my bedside table where I've been collecting all my toenails and bogies since I was about nought.

BOGIES & TOENAILS

'NOOOOO!!!' I screamed as it cracked open and the sky in my room filled up with little toenail-shaped moons and bogie-coloured planets.

'Look what you've done now!' I shouted, and one of the bogies landed on my tongue and I ate it.

Foot scrape

I picked up the remote control car and faced it towards Bunky, driving it full speed towards his ankle.

ROOAARR!

Because the whole carpet was covered in toenails and bogies though, the car was skidding everywhere and it ended up going between his stupid legs.

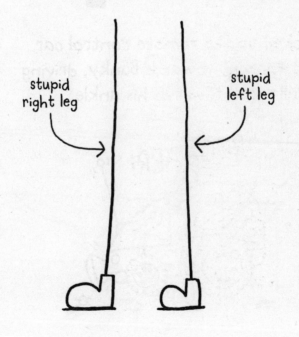

stupid
right leg

stupid
left leg

'Ha ha!' he laughed. 'I'm bored of this, I'm gonna watch **Future Ratboy!**' And he turned round and started walking downstairs like he owned the place, which he doesn't, I do.

'Oh no you don't, young man!' I said, marching after him in my bare feet, using my toes like fingers to collect bogies and nail clippings from the carpet.

Bunky was already back in the twizzle seat watching **Future Ratboy** when I got downstairs.

'Watch THIS!' I shouted, scraping the bottom of my foot down his face.

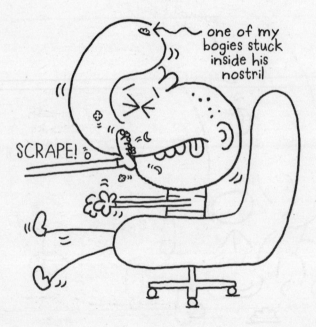

one of my bogies stuck inside his nostril

SCRAPE!

'ARRRGGGHHH, GET OFF ME!' he screamed, grabbing my ankle and flipping me on to the carpet, which could have killed me, so I did a massive groan and pretended to die right there and then on the spot.

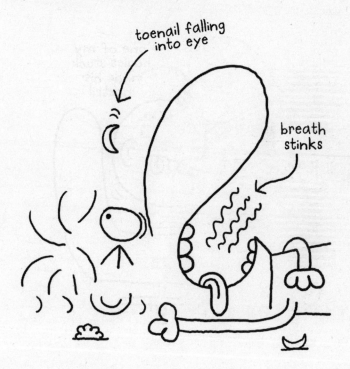

toenail falling into eye

breath stinks

'FOR CRYING OUT LOUD, WHAT'S GOING ON IN THERE?' shouted my mum from the kitchen.

'BARRY'S BULLYING ME!' shouted Bunky.

me

'BARRY, STOP BULLYING BUNKY!' shouted my dad.

'Right, that's it!' I screamed, coming back to life and standing up.

I glanced at the TV and saw **Future Ratboy** throwing a baddy through a window.

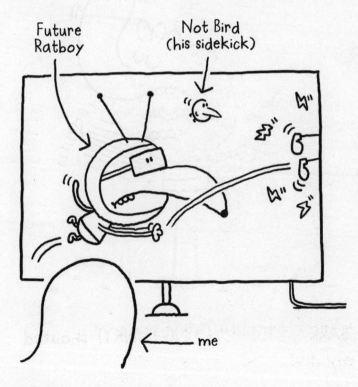

Future Ratboy

Not Bird (his sidekick)

← me

'GET OUT!' I shouted, dragging Bunky to the front door and pushing him into the road.

SHOVE!

'AND DON'T COME BACK!'

Being bored all on my own

After that I watched the rest of **Future Ratboy**, then got dressed and picked up all the bogies and fingernails off my bedroom carpet, then went back downstairs to see what was happening.

What was happening was that my mum was watching a black-and-white film with a cup of tea and a biscuit, and my dad was in the back garden carrying paving stones around with his tongue sticking out and his face all red.

I walked straight to the phone and dialled Bunky's number.

'GO,' said Bunky's voice, which is how we both answer the phone because that's how **Future Ratboy** does it.

'GET OVER HERE RIGHT NOW,' I shouted, then I hung up.

Five minutes later

'ARRRGGGHHH!!!' screamed my dad, dropping a paving stone on his foot, and my mum rushed out to give him a cup of tea and a cuddle.

Which was good, because it meant the TV was free for us to start watching **Future Ratboy** again when Bunky arrived.

'Sandwich?' I said, getting up and bumping past his chair so it twizzled round to face the wall.

SWIRL!

I chuckled to myself and patted Bunky on the head, glad to have my best friend back, even though he is the most annoying person in the whole entire world, amen.

'Ooh, yes please,' said Bunky, and I
walked into the kitchen, making us
both a sandwich.

Mine with cheese and pickle in it,
and his with toenails and bogies.

BOGIES &
TOENAILS

The end

Thank you for reading my v. short story. Please don't feed your best friend a toenail and bogie sandwich next time you see them.

Freaky Feeko's

Arrgghh!!! All the stuff in Feeko's Supermarket has gone invisible! Draw it back on the shelves, and make it dis-gus-ter-ing like Bunky's toenail and bogie sandwich!

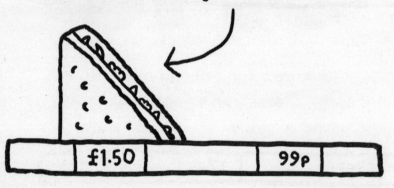

£1.50   99p

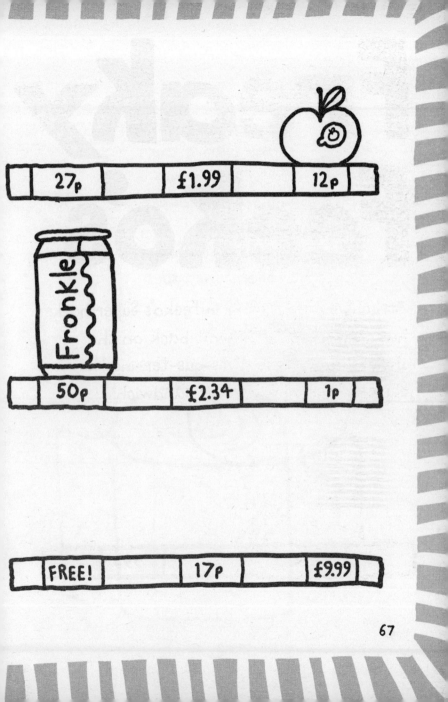

27p   £1.99   12p

Fronkle

50p   £2.34   1p

FREE!   17p   £9.99

Anton Mildew from
my class is the
editor of our
school newspaper,
The Daily Poo.
Here's a few pages
from one issue!

(printed on
recycled
toilet paper)
(not)

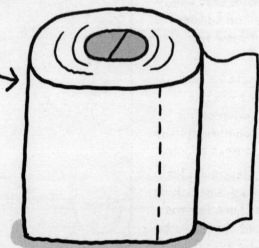

The Daily Poo

Edited by Anton Mildew

Invisible friend goes missing

Fay Snoggles reports

The invisible best buddy of Daily Poo Editor Anton Mildew has vanished.

'One minute he was there, the next he wasn't,' whimpered Mildew, pointing at the bit of air next to him.

Mildew, describing his see-through sidekick as 'always there for me', has asked the public to keep their eyes peeled for a floating can of Invisible Fronkle.

Anton and 'Invis' during better times

Ringpull shop to open

Darren Darrenofski

A shop selling just ring-pulls and nothing else is opening in Mogden, it has been revealed.

The shop, which will be called 'Ringpulls', will sell ringpulls, and maybe bottle tops as well, but they're not sure yet.

'I think it's great! You can only get ringpulls off of the tops of cans at the moment, which is annoying if you're not thirsty,' said Seymour Squelch, an avid ringpull collector and the person who is opening the shop.

Everyone else thinks it's a stupid idea, apart from me.

Nothing happens

Sharonella reports

Nothing happened again yesterday, which makes it three days in a row where nothing's happened. Hopefully something will happen today, but probably not.

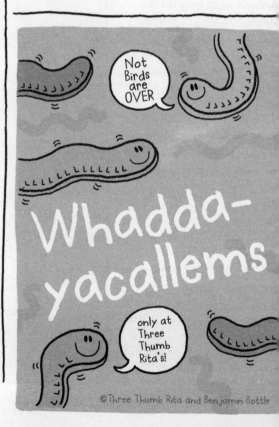

Not Birds are OVER

Whadda-yacallems

only at Three Thumb Rita's!

©Three Thumb Rita and Benjamin Bottle

My goldfish keeps changing what he looks like

by Anton Mildew

I don't get it. That's the third time my goldfish (Herman) has changed what he looks like COMPLETELY!

Yesterday he was fat and really old-looking, and he had one eye missing from when my cat (Bernadette) scooped him out of the tank last week. Now he's thin and looks half his age and has two eyes.

'It's a miracle, Mama!' I said to my mama, who I call Mama, not Mum.

'Please don't call me Mama, Anton. It's embarrassing. And I've seen the other mums laughing,' said Mama, and I patted her on her head.

'Oh Mama, you are funny!' I chortled, and I went back to staring at my fish. 'Isn't Mama a Silly Billy, Herman!' I smiled, and the bit of poo that'd been hanging out of his bum fell off and floated to the bottom of the tank.

Herman and his bit of poo. Sometimes he eats it.

Something happens

Sharonella reports

Something happened yesterday! That's why I'm writing this story about it.

OMG it was amazing! You wouldn't believe it even if I told you, which I am going to.

OK, right, well it was me and Tracy and Donnatella, and we were in the toilets when this THING just suddenly happened!

It was SO. WEIRD. And Tracy was like, 'You should write about this in The Daily Poo!' and Donnatella was behind her nodding her head, which is her way of saying 'You totally should do!'

Which is basically why I've done this story?

The end?

This is where it happened?

Granny stuck in photo

writes Jocelyn Twiggs

The family of a granny believed to be trapped inside a picture frame for three days were surprised to find that she'd just popped down the shops.

"It turns out she was at the supermarket all along!" laughed her grandson, Stuart Shmendrix.

just a photo

Edith Shmendrix, 98, is well known for her marathon pop-outs, once spending a week putting the milk bottles out.

Design your own paper

Here's what you've got to come up with:

1. a newspaper name

2. a headline for your story

3. then write the story

4. and draw a photo for it

NEWSPAPER

Headline

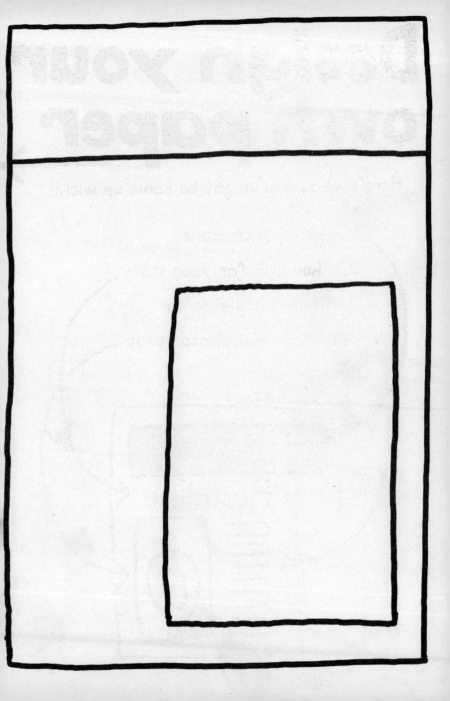

Knock Knock jokes!

Here are Not Bird's favourite NOT knock jokes! They're really rubbish!

Knock knock

Go away

78

WRITE YOUR OWN
REALLY RUBBISH
NOT KNOCK
JOKE HERE!

Ringpulls!

I like ringpulls. I just think they're keel.
So I always try and sneak drawings of
them into my books. Here are some,
turned into other things.
Because I'm keel.

glasses

someone
eating a
ringpull

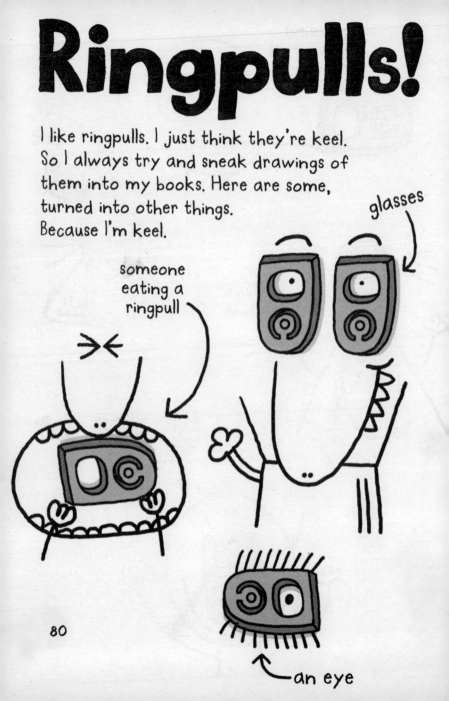

an eye

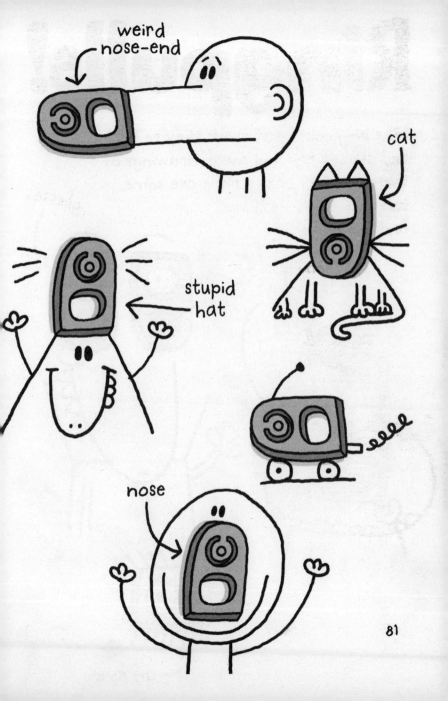

weird
nose-end

cat

stupid
hat

nose

81

your turn!

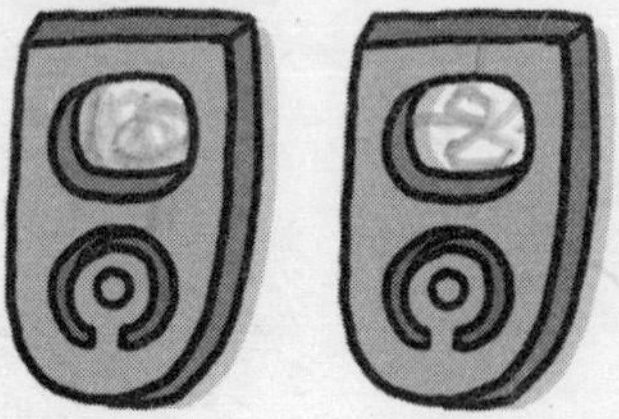

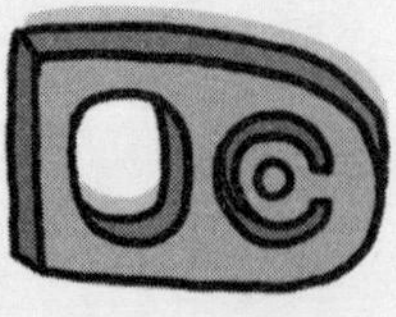

83

This is the book
I wrote for
World Book Day 2014. ⟶
It's all about insects.
And playing it keel.

AmazeKeel news

Probably the most exciting millisecond in the history of my whole entire life on earth amen was the other day after school when my mum called me into the kitchen.

don't know the news yet

BAARRRYYYY!!!

'Look at this!' she said, holding up the Mogden Gazette. 'Feeko's Supermarkets are bringing out a new shampoo and they're looking for three kids to be in the advert! You could audition with Bunky and Nancy!'

excited nose

I jumped in the air and did a dance, and my trousers fell down. Then I picked up the phone and dialled my best friend Bunky's number, which I'm jealous of because it's better than mine.

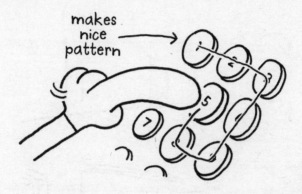

makes nice pattern →

'Bunky! Have you heard?' I screamed when he answered.

'What, have I heard your VOICE?' said Bunky, cracking up at his own stupid joke, but I just ignored him and carried on with what I was saying.

'No you complete loseroid, they're auditioning for a shampoo advert at Feeko's tomorrow!' I snortled, almost weeing myself with excitement.

Bunky

me

I was jiggling around the kitchen like my mum when she dances to the radio, probably because I actually did need a real-life wee really badly.

'Keel!' said Bunky, which is what me and Bunky say instead of 'cool', mostly because it's keeler, but also because it's what they say in our favourite TV show, Future Ratboy.

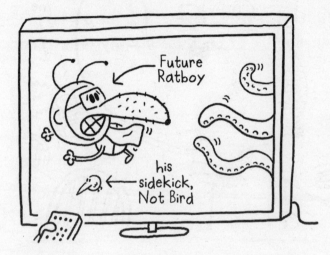

Future Ratboy

his sidekick, Not Bird

I hung up on Bunky and dialled Nancy Verkenwerken's number, which I'm also jealous of, but not as much as Bunky's.

'Nancy! Have you heard?' I said when she answered, except it wasn't Nancy, it was her dad.

'Nancy's round at Bunky's,' said Mr Verkenwerken, so I hung up and phoned Bunky again, jealous of his number AND because Nancy was there.

the wee wiggle

loserish phone cord

'WHAT'S NANCY DOING ROUND YOUR HOUSE WITHOUT ME?' I shouted when Bunky answered the phone, except it wasn't Bunky, it was Nancy.

'I popped in. I do live next door to him, you know,' said Nancy, but I just ignored her and carried on with what I was saying.

Nancy (obviously)

'Yeah, well, did he tell you the amazekeel news?' I said, stretching the phone cord so I could go for a wee in the toilet, which was across the hall from where I was standing in the kitchen.

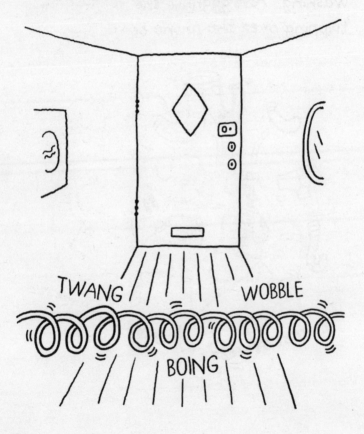

TWANG

WOBBLE

BOING

'Yeah, it's keel!' said Nancy, completely copying what me and Bunky say.

Suddenly and boringly my mum walked down the hall, carrying a pile of dirty washing. 'Arrrggghhh!' she screamed, tripping over the phone cord.

TRIP!

STRETCH

The phone flew out of my hand and I twizzled round like a ballerina. 'See you at Feeko's tomorrow morning. Eight o'clock sharp!' I shouted, wee going everywhere, not that I cared because I was going to be in a shampoo advert!

Best mood ever

The next morning I sprang out of bed like there was a spring springing me out of it. I looked at the mattress and saw a massive spring springing out of the sheet and realised that a real-life spring had actually sprung me out.

like the phone cord

I chuckled to myself, jumping into the shower with a spring in my step, thinking how it was the first day of spring, which is my favourite season ever, even though I hate the word 'spring' and try not to say it all that much if possible.

SHHHHHHHHHH

shower trying to stop me singing

Feeko's shampoo

'What's going on here?' said my mum when I came downstairs with my hair all washed and shiny. I think she was a bit surprised, seeing as I usually only have about one shower every eight million years.

'I have to look my best for the shampoo advert!' I said, and my mum did her smile she does when she thinks I'm the best son ever, which I am.

best son ever

'Ooh my snuggly little Snookyflumps!'
she warbled, giving me a cuddle, which I
wriggled out of, even though I secretly
quite liked it.

Then I skateboarded off to Feeko's
Supermarket, going extra fast because
of all the excitement-turbo-blowoffs
I was doing.

What a lovely day

'Barry!' shouted Bunky as I skateboarded up to Feeko's playing it keel times a billion and three-quarters. He was halfway down the queue of kids, which was caterpillaring round the building like one of those long wriggly insect things I can never remember the name of.

'You made it!' I smiled, my hair glistening in the sunshine. Nancy strolled up and picked a flower that was growing out of a crack in the pavement, and I gave her a triple-reverse-upside-down-salute, which is what I do when I'm in the best mood ever.

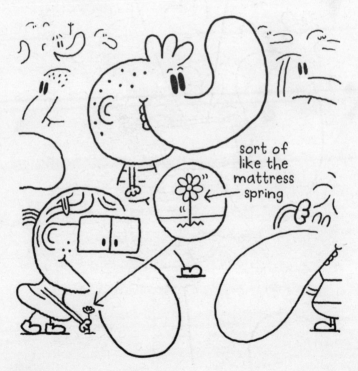

sort of like the mattress spring

'Lovely day, isn't it!' she beamed,
sniffing on the flower and sneezing
into my face. The sun was beaming in
the sky even more than Nancy, and
Bunky pulled out a pair of **Future
Ratboy** sunglasses.

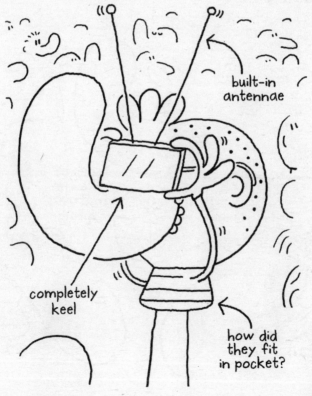

built-in
antennae

completely
keel

how did
they fit
in pocket?

'Oh. My. Days. I am LUVVING your shades, Bunky!' said an annoying voice from behind me that sounded just like Sharonella's from our class at school.

I turned round and did a blowoff out of shock, because it actually WAS Sharonella, not that I should have been all that surprised, seeing as the voice had sounded EX-ACK-ER-LY like hers.

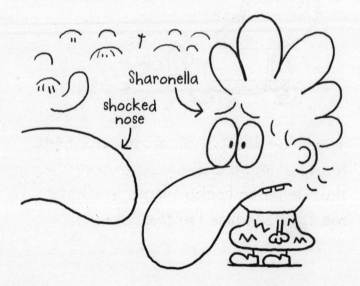

Sharonella

shocked nose

'Helloooo, Darren fans!' said Darren Darrenofski, who I hadn't spotted because he was standing behind Sharonella, and I did another blowoff because of how annoying he is too.

Darren

crocodile face

can of Fronkle

'Next five kids!' shouted a spotty fat man holding a clipboard, and we shuffled into Feeko's Supermarket, me first because I'm the best.

The store room

'This way,' shouted the clipboard man, walking us through Feeko's, which was full of grannies and grandads doing their boring old Saturday morning shopping.

Right at the back of the store was an enormous metal door with a yellow poster on it saying 'Nit Shampoo Auditions Here!'

'Nit shampoo? You didn't say it was for NIT SHAMPOO!' said Bunky, pointing at the poster, then poking me in the nose with the finger he'd just been pointing at the poster with.

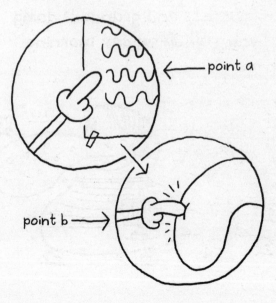

point a

point b

'Oh well, we're here now!' I smiled, thinking how I should be in a good mood more often, and I pushed the door open and walked through.

We were in the storeroom, which was like a whole nother Feeko's, except much colder and without any customers. It had all the same stuff stacked up in cardboard boxes, on shelves eight million times the height of normal ones.

The clipboard man walked us over to the shampoo aisle and told us to wait there, then walked off again, his footsteps echoing.

It was boring just standing there waiting, so I stuck my hand into a cardboard box and pulled out a bottle of Feeko's Cherry Shampoo.

I covered the 'SHAM' bit with my finger
and put on my advert face. 'Mmm,
Feeko's Cherry poo!' I snortled, and
Bunky and Nancy weed themselves
with laughter.

'That boy! The one with the hair!'
growled a voice out of nowhere, and
I spotted a man with an unlit cigar
hanging out of his mouth, pointing at
me. 'He's perfect!'

that man I was just talking about

I'm not used to people saying I'm perfect, so I jumped in the air and did a dance, and my trousers fell down. 'Little old keelness me?' I smiled, copying what **Future Ratboy** said when he won 'Keelest Person Ever' on the TV Awards last year.

The clipboard man walked over and bent down. 'The director would like to see you first,' he whispered in my ear, his voice going right through my brain and out the other ear, into one of Nancy's.

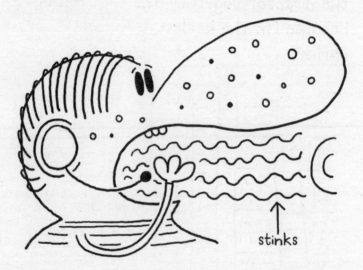

stinks

'What about me and Bunky?' Nancy said, looking all sad.

I looked over at my best friends and felt sorry for them for not being as brilliant as me.

'I don't go anywhere without these two!' I said, and we walked over to the director together, me first again, because I'm the keelest, like I said earlier.

Feeko's Nit Shampoo

'Names?' said a frizzy-haired woman standing next to the director. Nancy and Bunky said their names, which are 'Nancy Verkenwerken' and 'Bunky' in case you didn't know.

'Barry Loser,' I said, smiling like I was in an advert for being Barry Loser.

'Barry Loser? That's hilarious!' chuckled the director, and everyone laughed, including Darren and Sharonella, who were standing at the edge waiting for their go.

clipboard man

I snortled, feeling like I was in one of those dreams where everything's going really well, and the frizzy-haired woman nudged us into the middle of the aisle.

'Just walk a bit, as if you're going down the street . . .' she said, looking at my hair all jealously.

I glanced at Bunky, who's sort of like my pet dog, then at Nancy, who's sort of like my pet cat, which sort of made me their leader, which meant I'd better say something.

'Bunky, Nancy,' I said, putting my arms round them, 'let's give this a hundred and twenty million billion percent!' I whispered, copying what they say on my mum's favourite TV talent show. I put my hand up and we all high fived, and it echoed round the storeroom.

← high three more like

Nancy started to stroll, twiddling her flower and looking up at the ceiling lights as if they were the sun. 'What a lovely day!' she beamed.

'Yes, isn't it glorious!' I said, glancing up at the fake sun and snatching Bunky's **Future Ratboy** sunglasses off his face. 'If only I didn't have these pesky nits in my hair . . .'

GRAB!

The director chuckled and the frizzy-haired woman jotted something down in her notebook.

'Can't . . . see . . .' mumbled Bunky, squinting from his no sunglasses. He stumbled into a shelf and a cardboard box crashed to the floor, shampoo bottles flying everywhere.

CRASH!

'Hmmm . . .' grumbled the director, and the frizzy-haired woman jotted something else down in her notebook, but not in a good way. I bent over, worried Bunky was ruining everything, and picked up a bottle of almond conditioner.

pretending he's dead so I don't pick him up

'Ooh, Feeko's Nit Shampoo,' I said, totally making it up on the spot. 'Just the thingypoos for my nit problem!'

I flipped the lid open, held it over my head and squeezed. Light-brown slime drizzled on to my hair and down my face.

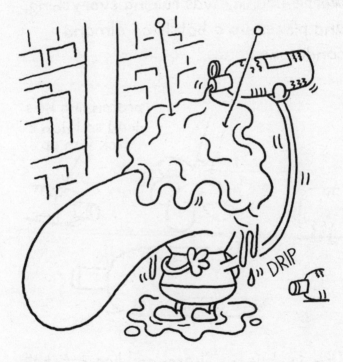

DRIP

'Feeko's Nit Shampoo,' I said, doing my best advert voice. 'Because it's keel!'

There was a millisecond of silence like you get in-between adverts on the telly, then the director stood up.

'Bravo!' he roared, and everyone in the whole shampoo aisle applauded, including me, because I'm my number-one fan.

CLAP!
CLAP!
CLAP!
CLAP!
CLAP!

Even more amazekeel news

After that we sat through seven billion other auditions which were all completely rubbish, including Sharonella and Darren's.

Yay, shampoo!

Yeah, yay

Then the director whispered something into the frizzy-haired woman's ear and she clapped her hands, but not like she was clapping someone, more to shut us up.

normal clap   shush clap

'Thank you all for coming today. It's been SO hard to decide!' she shouted, which is what they always say at things like this, just to make the losers feel better. 'However, the three winners have been chosen, and they are ... Barry Loser, Nancy Verkenwerken and Bunky!'

You know how I said the most exciting millisecond in the history of my whole entire life on earth amen was when my mum told me about the shampoo auditions? That was until right now.

'YIPPEE-KEEL-KAYAY!' I screamed, jumping in the air with Nancy and Bunky, and we all did a dance, and my trousers fell down.

shampoo wiped off

A week later

It was a week later and my mum was dropping me, Bunky and Nancy off to film the advert.

'See you later for your big camping trip!' said my mum, because we were sleeping in the tent in my back garden that night to celebrate being famous.

TRUNDLE

'OK, Mrs Bunky!' I shouted, pretending she was Bunky's mum because of how embarrassing she is, and she ruffled my hair.

The advert was being filmed down the poshest street in Mogden, which was sort of like the shampoo aisle in Feeko's storeroom except the cardboard boxes were enormous houses, and instead of fake sun there was cloud.

Darren Darrenofski wobbled up, sipping on a can of Fronkle. 'Good mornkeels, Darren fans!' he burped, and I spotted something Sharonella-ish behind him.

'What in the name of unkeelness are YOU TWO doing here?' I said, patting my hair down where my mum had just ruffled it.

'We're spectatoring!' said Sharonella, and I felt sorry for them, not being the stars of a nit shampoo advert like me.

Darren's nose

Sharonella's whole head

my nose

The director walked over and ruffled my hair right where I'd just patted it down.

'Hey kids! I had the greatest idea for the advert last night,' he said, all excitedly. 'It's got everything – energy, passion, FIZZAZZ!'

fizzazz

'What IS it?' said Sharonella, even though it was none of her business.

'One word: ROLLER SKATES!' he boomed, and I gulped, because I'd never roller skated in my life.

'That's two words,' said Nancy, and I trod on her foot to shut her up.

'One, two, what's the difference?' breathed the director, blowing a cloud of cigar smoke into my face.

mixed with really bad breath

FFFFFFFFF

I thought about my skateboard, and
how roller skating is probably just like
riding two skateboards instead of one.

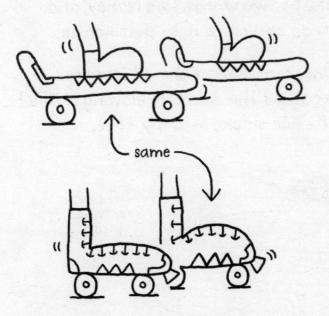

same

'Yeah Nancy, what's the difference?' I
said, and she trod on BOTH my feet to
shut me up.

Runaway Loser

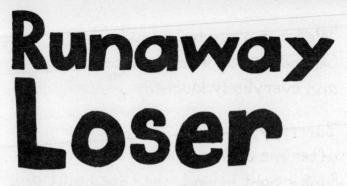

Frizzy hair gave us all a pair of roller skates and a helmet each. I put mine on and stood up.

You know how I said the advert was being filmed on the poshest street in Mogden? It's also the hilliest.

'Waaaahhhhh!!!' I screamed, rolling backwards down a huge slope.

ZOOM!

'We have a runaway Loser,' said
Clipboard man into a walkie-talkie,
and everybody laughed.

'Barrrryyyy!' cried Nancy, zooming
after me on her roller skates, with
Bunky right behind. They sped past and
looped back, stretching their arms out
and holding hands to catch me.

'Uunnggfh!' I blurted, crashing into them, and we all fell over.

I stood up, wobblingly, and patted my hair down for the eight millionth time that morning, even though it was inside a helmet. 'Let's film this advert!' I boomed, trying to sound like their leader, and I fell straight down on my bum again.

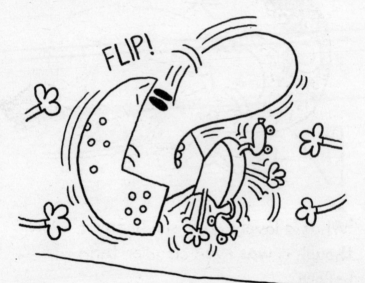

FLIP!

Action

'Aaaaannnnddd . . . ACTION!' boomed the director, and Nancy started to roller skate down the road.

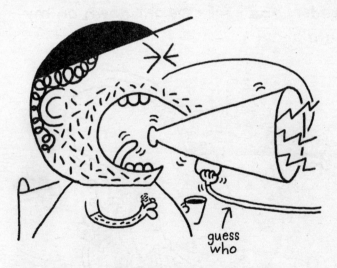

guess
who

'What a lovely day!' she beamed, even though it was even cloudier than before.

'Isn't it glorious!' I warbled, wobbling behind her, my arms waggling to keep steady. 'If only I didn't have these pesky nits doing poos all over my head.' I rolled past the camera and crashed into the frizzy-haired woman.

two seconds before crash

'CUT!' growled the director. 'Barry baby, where's the magic gone?' he said, blowing cigar smoke in my face AGAIN.

A huge black cloud had appeared behind him, and I imagined a giant director out in space, blowing cigar smoke on to the world.

the world

instead of moon

I tried to stand up, but my feet were skidding off in opposite directions. Bunky and Nancy rolled over and dragged me to the kerb. 'You OK, Barry?' said Nancy, and I gave her a thumbs up, mostly because I was too out of breath to speak.

'OK, let's go again,' shouted the director. 'Really work it this time, guys. Aaaaannnnddd . . . ACTION!'

'What a LUVVERLY day!' said Nancy, and Bunky twizzled round like a ballerina.

'Isn't it glorious!' I said, zooming past them and tripping over a camera wire. 'ARRGGHHH!!!' I screamed, flying through the air and landing in a bush.

'Maybe we could get rid of the roller skates?' I heard the frizzy-haired woman say to the director, her voice muffled from all the leaves around my ears.

The air had turned cold, like in the storeroom at Feeko's.

'What, and lose the FIZZAZZ?!' growled the director. He looked at his watch, then the big black cloud, and shook his head.

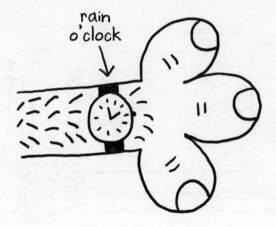

rain o'clock

139

'Is there anyone else here who can roller skate?' asked the director.

'Me!' shouted Darren Darrenofski before I'd even clambered out of the bush.

LEAP!

Thunder and lightning

'Help me!' I wailed, trying to get up, my feet running away from their owner, who was me.

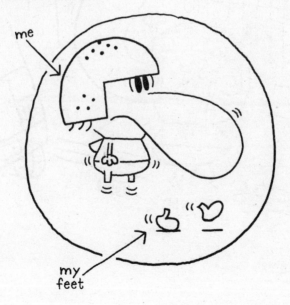

me

my feet

Darren was squidging his fat little feet
into a spare pair of roller skates as
Bunky and Nancy glided towards me.
They grabbed a Barry-arm each and
rolled me over to the director.

'You've got to give him one more
chance!' said Nancy, holding me up like
an old grandad who can't walk.

Lightning struck in the distance as Darren trundled past doing a little jump. 'Barry baby, what can I tell you,' sighed the director. 'I've gotta get this thing filmed before the rain starts. I'm sorry, really I am.'

RUMBLE

My knees gave way and I collapsed to the floor like an empty Feeko's carrier bag. 'But you said I was perfect!' I cried.

I lay on the ground, thinking how this whole auditioning thing had been my idea in the first place.

'BUNKY, NANCY, I ORDER YOU NOT TO BE IN THE NIT SHAMPOO ADVERT WITHOUT YOUR LEADER!' I roared, but in a nice way, and waited for them both to say 'OK' and take off their roller skates.

CRACK!

Bunky looked at me all guiltily, like a dog just before it's about to do a poo right in the middle of the pavement.

naughty Bunky

Nancy glided over, her ponytail swishing like a cat's tail. She held my hand in hers and looked me in the eyes, then glanced towards the director.

BZZZ—

'I'm so sorry, Barry,' she said, turning round and floating away, and I did the angriest blowoff in the history of angry blowoffs ever. Or maybe it was just the thunder.

The long walk home

It was a long walk home in the rain from the posh street to my house, especially with Sharonella bobbling along next to me for half of it, going on about how we were the only two people not in a nit shampoo advert.

'Forget about that lot, Barry. Who needs 'em, that's what I say!' she wheezed, huffing and puffing to keep up, but I just ignored her and carried on with what I was doing.

I was soaking wet by the time I got to my front door. 'What's happened to my Snookyflumps?' chuckled my mum as the clouds parted and the sun came out behind me.

I barged past her up to my bedroom and started packing my rucksack. 'Barrypoos, are you OK?' she warbled, her knees clicking as she climbed the stairs.

I grabbed my cuddly **Future Ratboy** and stuffed him into the bag, looking out the window at the tent that me, Bunky and Nancy were supposed to be camping in tonight, to celebrate being famous.

'Where are Bunky and Nancy?' said my mum, and I thought of them celebrating with Darren, somewhere else.

I swung the rucksack over my shoulder and stomped downstairs, straight towards the tent.

'SEE YOU IN A MILLION YEARS,' I shouted to everyone in the whole wide world, and I zipped the floppy door shut behind me.

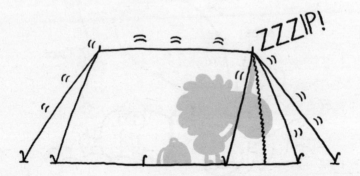

ZZZIP!

Camping on my ownypoos

I lay down on my sleeping bag and closed my eyes, trying to forget about it all, and felt something tickle my face.

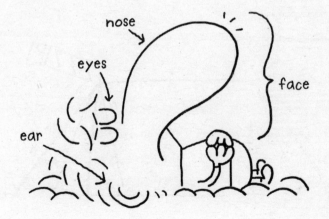

nose

eyes

ear

face

'ARRRGGGHHH! SPIDER!' I screamed, unzipping the door and rolling on to the wet grass. I scrabbled at my nose, which was where the tickle was, and a sleeping bag feather floated off it, into the sky.

I tutted to myself, crawling back inside the tent, and lay down with my head sticking out like a dog in his kennel. The whole garden was glistening now, sun reflecting off the wet leaves and into my eyes.

One of those insect things with seven trillion legs trundled past, smiling. 'What are YOU so happy about?' I mumbled.

Three centimetres away an ant was busy dragging his dead ant-friend down a tiny little hole in the earth.

'You wouldn't abandon YOUR leader, would you, Mr Ant?' I whispered to him in my best insect voice.

I looked around at all the millions of other insects pottering about, minding their own businesses, and thought how sweet they were, eating leaves and doing the tiniest poos ever.

And then it hit me.

What had I been thinking, wanting to be in a Feeko's Nit Shampoo advert? I wasn't an insect murderer!

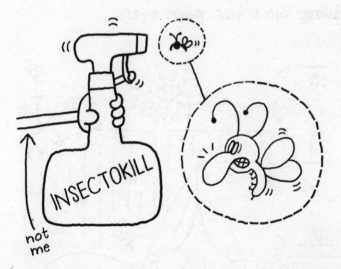

Who did Nancy and Bunky reckon they were, roller skating around with Darren Darrenofski, telling people to kill innocent little bugs!

'Snackypoos, Snookyflumps!' chirped my mum, knocking on the tent and passing me a plate of chocolate digestives. 'Bunky and Nancy phoned ... I said you'd call them when you were ready.'

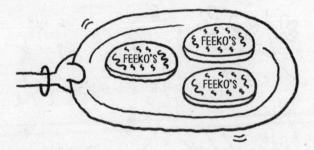

I looked at the Feeko's logo stamped into the biscuits, and thought of my evil insect-killing ex-best-friends with their keeler-than-mine phone numbers, starring in their stupid nit shampoo advert.

'Fanks, Mumsy,' I said, taking a bite of one, and twelve billion crumbs scattered on to the grass. 'Who needs 'em!' I whispered in my insect voice, settling down to dinner with my millions of tiny new best friends.

Insect
murderers

All of a non-sudden it was Monday and I was skateboarding to school through Mogden Common, which is this massive bit of grass in the middle of town where everyone takes their dogs to do poos.

TREMBLE

A butterfly was flitter-fluttering next to my head like a miniature fan, his tiny wings cooling me off in the morning sun, when I spotted a worm wriggling across the pavement.

'EEEKK!' I shrieked, swerving to miss him and crashing nose-first into a billboard.

'FEEKO'S NIT SHAMPOO KILLS NITS DEAD!'
said the headline on the poster.
Underneath there was a photo of
Bunky, Nancy and Darren roller skating
down the road, looking all happy and
nit-free.

'Insect murderers!' I grumbled, standing
up, and a fly flew right into my eyeball,
completely and utterly blinding me.

'Good!' I mumbled, because I didn't have to look at that stupid advert any more. Then I realised it wasn't good, because I'd accidentally killed a fly.

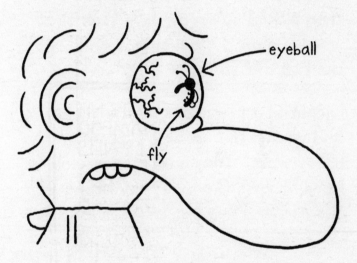

eyeball

fly

I rubbed my eye and looked into my hand. The fly was curled up, drowned in my tears, his little wings stuck to his body like my clothes after that walk home in the rain the other day.

'I'm sorry, Mr Fly,' I said, kneeling down and scraping a hole in the dirt. I plopped him in and put the dirt back, then picked up an old lolly stick that was lying on the pavement and broke the end off to make a gravestone.

I grabbed a pencil out of my rucksack and wrote 'FLY' in tiny capitals on the bit of wood. 'May you rest in keelness,' I said, digging the mini gravestone into the dirt and heading off for school.

Nits are the Keelest

The annoying thing about being the nicest, most non-insect-killing person in the whole wide world amen is that you have to stop every two minutes to bury all the insects you keep accidentally killing.

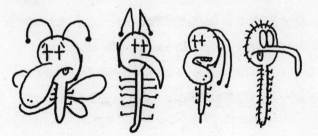

Like the ant I ran over with my skateboard three seconds after I'd drowned that fly in my eyeball. And the daddy-long-legs I swallowed while yawning eight milliseconds after that.

By the time I got to school I'd had to do so many insect funerals that I'd used up four lolly sticks and my pencil lead was completely worn down.

There was a crowd around Bunky and Nancy as I walked through the classroom door, everyone asking them about the advert and whether they were millionaires yet.

walking through door (get it?) →

'Barry!' said Bunky, walking over to me all guiltily like a dog that's just done a wee in the middle of the living room carpet.

'How are you, Barry?' said Nancy,
coming over and curling her arm round
my shoulder, but I just ignored her and
carried on with what I was doing.

'I had a word with the director about
the next advert. He said we could do it
on skateboards!' smiled Bunky, as if we
were still best friends, and I mouthed
'Yay!' and waggled my hands all
sarcastically.

doesn't
realise
I'm being
sarcastic

sarcastic
waggling

I flumped down at my desk and started drawing insects in my notebook. 'I don't want to be in your evil nit-murdering adverts,' I mumbled, writing 'NITS ARE THE KEELEST' in my best capitals at the top of a new page.

Just then, Darren barged through the classroom doors on his roller skates. 'Helloooo, Darren fans!' he burped, holding up a phone and pressing play on the screen.

ROLL

I squinted my eyes and saw him, Bunky and Nancy gliding down the posh street, high fiving each other and acting like they were the keelest people ever. 'FEEKO'S NIT SHAMPOO KILLS NITS DEAD!' growled a voice at the end of the advert, and everyone cheered.

'What are you cheering for? I shouted, scraping my chair and standing up. 'These people are murdering innocent nits!' I sat back down and drew a woodlouse, my hand shaking from how angry I was.

'He's gone stark raving bonkers!' laughed Darren, pressing play on the phone screen to make the advert start again. 'If anyone wants my autograph, I'm signing people's faces this lunchtime in the playground!'

A fly that'd been buzzing against the classroom window bonked his nose straight into the glass one last time and fell to the floor, dead from nose-bonk. I rolled my eyes, snapping a mini gravestone off a lolly stick in my pocket.

'Psst! Barry!' whispered Sharonella as I bent down to pick up the fly. 'I know you've gone mad and everything but I just wanted to say that I'm there for you, OK?'

I wasn't listening to her though. I was too busy coming up with one of my brilliant and amazekeel plans.

BZZZ ~

Give a bug a hug

The queue for autographs caterpillared all the way round the playground like one of those insects with twenty trillion legs I can never remember the name of.

171

'One at a time, Darren fans!' burped Darren, signing Fay Snoggles's nose, and Bunky snortled, scribbling his stupid name in someone's autograph book underneath Nancy's.

'Ready?' I said to Sharonella, taking a deep breath and accidentally breathing in a mosquito.

'Huh? Oh yeah, I was born ready!' said Sharonella, who was standing next to me picking her nose and holding a poster with 'NITS ARE PEOPLE TOO!' written on it.

I looked at my poster, which said 'GIVE A BUG A HUG' in my biggest capitals, patted myself on the back for coming up with such a brilliant and amazekeel idea, and started marching towards my ex-best-friends.

'Ban Feeko's Nit Shampoo!' I shouted, waving my poster in the air and hitting a ladybird but not killing it, so that's OK.

'GIVE-A-BUG-A-HUG,' burped Darren, reading my poster out loud. 'OK!' he snortled, running towards a daddy-long-legs that was flying past, minding its own business. 'Come to daddy, Daddy!' he snarfled, grabbing it by the wings and giving it a cuddle.

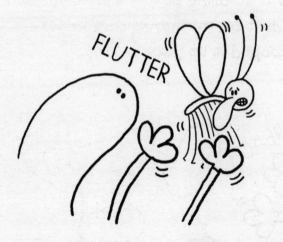

FLUTTER

'NOOO!!!' I screamed, dropping my poster and running towards him. Darren opened his arms and the daddy-long-legs dropped to the floor, all dizzy. 'You almost killed him!' I cried, stroking its wings, and it floated off, a bit wobbly.

'Oh no, I'm about to tread on an anty-want!' said Darren in a baby voice, lifting his foot above an ant that was strolling past. I scrabbled towards it on my hands and knees and scooped it up just in time.

REACH

The ground shook as Darren's foot stomped on to the floor, or maybe it was Mrs Dongle the school secretary bounding over.

WOBBLE

THUD!

'Boys, boys, I cannot tolerate this tomfoolery!' she wheezed, the wooden beads on her necklace knocking against each other.

'He started it!' burped Darren, opening a can of Fronkle and slurping it down in one go.

me

Mrs Dongle looked at me, lying on the floor holding an ant, then over at my poster. 'GIVE A BUG A HUG,' she said, reading it out loud. 'That's perfect!'

Mrs Dongle's office

It was ten minutes later and I was in Mrs Dongle's office, but not because I'd been naughty or anything.

'Have you heard about Mogden Common, Barry?' she smiled, offering me a chocolate digestive.

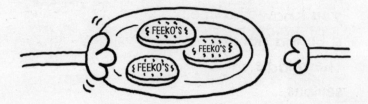

'Yes,' I said, but it came out as 'Mmf' because of the chocolate digestive I'd just stuffed in my mouth. 'It's that bit of grass where all the dogs do their poos,' I mumbled, spraying crumbs all over her desk.

Mogden Common

'That's it!' she chuckled. 'It's one of the last natural parts of Mogden left. Did you know that Feeko's wants to build a brand new mini supermarket right in the middle of it?' she said, suddenly all serious.

I thought of Mogden Common and remembered Mr Fly, lying in his tiny grave. 'I HATE Feeko's,' I said, looking out the window at Bunky and Nancy, acting all keel because of their stupid Feeko's advert.

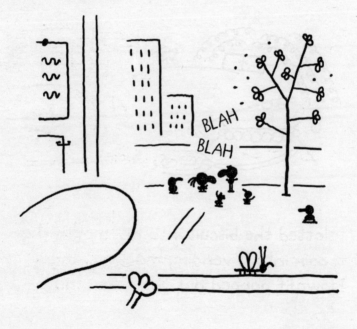

'There's a protest march coming up to stop them building it,' said Mrs Dongle, passing me another digestive, and I started to realise why the ground shook when she ran. 'Your posters would add just the FIZZAZZ we need!'

I slotted the biscuit into my mouth like a coin into a vending machine, and a blowoff popped out the other end.

The Feeko's protest

I spent the whole rest of the week
making posters for Mrs Dongle, and
burying insects I'd accidentally killed,
and not telling Sharonella about the
Feeko's protest, otherwise she'd want
to come too.

Then all of a non sudden it was Saturday and I was standing on the edge of Mogden Common with Mrs Dongle and all her wooden-bead-necklace friends and their husbands, wondering how in the unkeelness my life had ended up so loserish.

'Boo Feeko's!' growled an old granny, doddering past with a pram full of sausage dogs. She pulled a tied-up plastic bag out of her pocket and threw it at the enormous billboard that had been put up the day before.

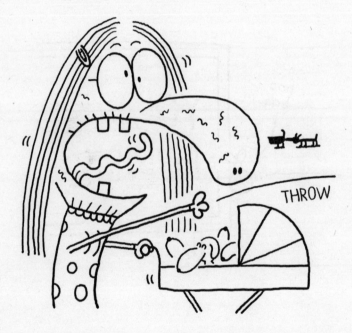

THROW

'YOUR NEW FEEKO'S FUNSIZE WILL BE HERE SOON!' said the billboard in the biggest capitals ever, and I wondered if me and Mrs Dongle's friends were wasting our time with our tiny little posters.

'Yes, that's right, Boo Feeko's!' shouted Mrs Dongle, waving her poster. On it I'd written 'FEEKO'S IS FOR LOSERS', which wasn't my most genius idea ever, but she seemed to like it.

A van with a satellite dish on the roof and 'Mogden TV' written on its side screeched up. A man with a camera jumped out, followed by a lady with blonde hair and a microphone.

'We are live at Mogden Common, where a riot has broken out in protest against the new Feeko's Funsize!' she said, flicking her fringe like me when I had my bouncy hair for the audition.

I looked around at all the Mrs Dongles and their husbands, standing there eating sandwiches and drinking tea, and wondered if this was what being in a riot was like.

Over on the other corner of the common, three figures started to glide towards us. One looked like a dog crossed with a human, the other had a cat's tail growing out of her head, and the third was half crocodile, half fat little belly.

I zoomed my eyes in and realised it was Bunky, Nancy and Darren, out practising their roller skating for the next evil nit-killing shampoo advert.

GLIDE ✻~

The cameraman swivelled round and started to film. 'This is verrry interesting,' said the blonde lady. 'It seems the stars of the huuuugely successful Feeko's Nit Shampoo advert have turned up. Who knows what could happen next?'

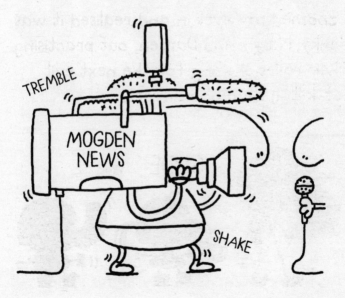

TREMBLE

MOGDEN NEWS

SHAKE

What happened next

'It's those nit shampoo kids!' shouted the old granny, giving her pram a push and letting go.

It zoomed off like me on roller skates, slicing a worm in half with one of its wheels. 'Get 'em, boys!' she cackled, and the dogs leaped out of the pram and ran towards Bunky like a string of sausages.

'ARRGGHHH!!!' screamed Bunky, who's COM-PER-LEET-ER-LY scared of dogs. He twizzled round to zoom off and fell straight down on his bum. The sausage dogs swarmed round him, wagging their tails and yapping.

not really a sausage

YAP!

WAG!

Mrs Dongle dropped her poster and bounded over. 'Bad doggies, naughty pooches!' she warbled, the TV people right behind her.

'Tell us how you're feeling!' said the blonde lady, stuffing her microphone into Bunky's face.

'My bum hurts,' said Bunky, a sausage dog licking his face.

I tiptoed over and watched from behind my poster, hoping they wouldn't see me.

192

'Well, well, if it isn't Barry Loser!' burped Darren, spotting me straight away, probably because of my massive nose sticking out from behind the poster. 'How many ants have you snogged today?' he laughed.

new helmet

DAZZER!

The camera swung round to me and I felt myself go the colour of a bottle of Feeko's Cherry Shampoo.

'How many have you KILLED, insect murder?' I shouted, waving my poster and hitting a daddy-long-legs but not killing it, so that's OK.

'None yet, but it's never too late!' said Darren, grabbing a fly that was flying past, and all the Mrs Dongles and their husbands gasped.

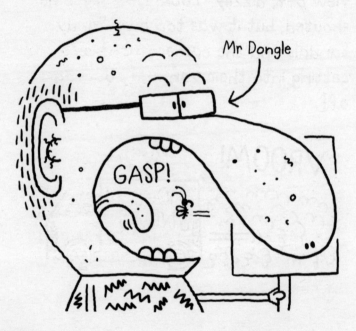

Mr Dongle

'Truly shocking scenes here at Mogden Common,' said the blonde lady into the camera. 'That was one of the stars of the Feeko's Nit Shampoo advert happily murdering a fly, just for the fun of it. This is Sandy Sandals for Mogden News Tonight!'

Darren opened his hand and the fly flew off, dizzily. 'Look! He's alive!' he shouted, but it was too late. Sandy Sandals and the cameraman were getting into their van and zooming off.

The news

'Bazza, have you heard?!' screamed Sharonella as I skateboarded through the school gates on Monday morning.

'What, have I heard your VOICE?' I said, chuckling to myself about my own joke, not that I was in much of a chuckling mood.

'No, the news about Darren!'

I flipped my skateboard up and took
my helmet off, scratching my head
because all of a sudden I'd been feeling
a bit itchy.

'Feeko's fired him!' snortled Sharonella.
'Nancy and Bunky too! They saw what
Darren did on Mogden News and said
they couldn't have insect murderers
in their nit shampoo adverts!'

I was just about to do my dance that makes my trousers fall down when I spotted Bunky walking through the school gates with Nancy and Darren.

'I suppose you're happy now, aren't you,' mumbled Bunky all sadly, scratching his head.

'Not really,' I mumbled back, because I wasn't really. I still hadn't been in a Feeko's Nit Shampoo advert, plus I didn't have any friends apart from Sharonella and the insects, not that they counted if I was being honest, which I was.

CLANG! CLONK! DONK!

CLANK! CLUNK!

The sound of wooden beads clanging against each other floated into my ears and I turned round and saw Mrs Dongle.

'Have you heard the news, Barry?' she warbled, and I scratched my head while shaking it. 'Our little protest was a complete waste of time. Didn't do anything! They're still going to build that ghastly Feeko's Funsize!'

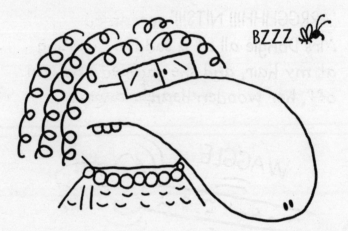

BZZZ

I did my sad face, mostly just to make Mrs Dongle happy, and carried on standing there, scratching my head. And then it happened.

Nits

'ARRGGHHH!!! NITS!!!' screamed
Mrs Dongle all of a sudden, pointing
at my hair, and she jumped and ran
off, her wooden beads clanging.

WAGGLE

'What is it? WHAT IS IT?' I cried, even
though Mrs Dongle had said what it
was.

Sharonella tiptoed over and peered into my hair. 'OH. MY. DAYS! Barry, you've got like a kazillion nits!' she said, squirming away from me and running off, screaming.

ZOOM!

I reached out to Nancy, forgetting we weren't friends any more, which is what happens when you're too busy worrying about all the nits eating away at your brain.

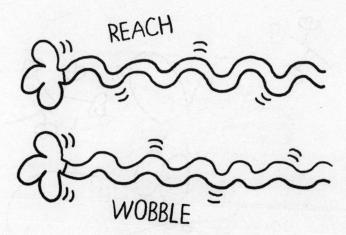

REACH

WOBBLE

'Nancy, you've got to help me!' I wailed, my legs and arms flailing.

Nancy slinked away from me, scratching her head, and I zoomed my eyes in and spotted the most nit-looking thing I've ever seen, going for a morning stroll along her eyebrow.

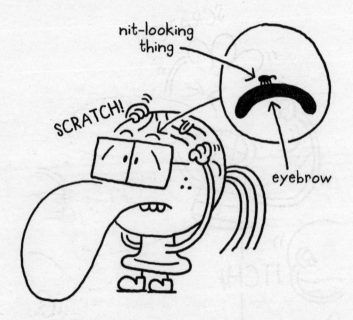

nit-looking thing

SCRATCH!

eyebrow

'ARRGGHHH!!! NITS!!!' I screamed, pointing at Nancy, and she started scratching and flailing, just like me.

'ARRGGHHH!!! NITS!!!' screamed Darren all of a sudden, pointing at Bunky's hair, and Bunky joined in with me and Nancy, itching himself like a dog.

'ARRGGHHH!!! NITS!!!' screamed Bunky, pointing at Darren, and that was how me, Bunky, Nancy and Darren all ended up standing in a circle doing the scratchy nit dance.

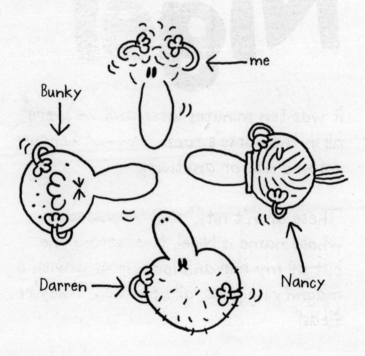

Bunky

me

Darren

Nancy

Nurse Nigel

It was ten minutes later and we were all in the nurse's room, but not because we had nits or anything.

'These aren't nits,' said the nurse, whose name is Nigel, tweezering one out of my ear and looking at it with a magnifying glass, all confused. 'They're fleas!'

I glanced over at Bunky, then Nancy, but not at Darren, because I don't really like looking at him all that much.

'The sausage dogs!' I laughed, remembering how one of them had been really scratching his bum with his mouth just before he'd licked Bunky's face.

Bunky's nose

flea

that dog

'Most extraordinary,' mumbled Nurse Nigel to himself. He opened his cupboard door and peered in, scratching his chin, but not because he had fleas or anything. 'Here we go!' he smiled, pulling out a big plastic bottle with 'Feeko's Flea Shampoo for Dogs' written on it in massive non-capitals.

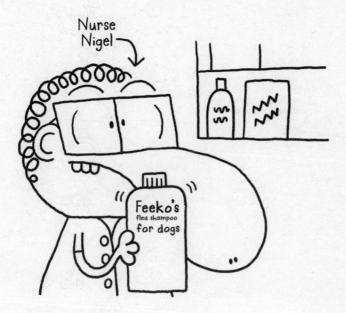

Nurse Nigel

Feeko's
flea shampoo
for dogs

So that's how I ended up in the school showers with Bunky, Nancy and Darren, stripped to my **Future Ratboy** vest and pants and covered in Feeko's Flea Shampoo for Dogs.

SHHHHHHHHH

Feeko's Flea Shampoo for Dogs

'Do us a favour Barry,' burped Darren, foam and dead fleas running down his belly. 'Next time she goes on a protest, tell your mum not to bring her sausage dogs!' he snortled, and Nancy and Bunky giggled, trying not to laugh out loud.

foam bubble

dead flea

'She's YOUR mum, not mine!' I shouted, looking down at all the dead fleas floating in the water, feeling a bit bad because I'd gone back to being an insect killer like my evil ex-best-friends.

'Get 'em, boys!' shrieked Nancy, doing her impression of the old granny with the pram, and I snortled to myself then stopped, because I was still angry with Bunky and Nancy for abandoning their leader.

looks like a toilet plunger taking off

'I'm sorry Barry, real-keely I am,' said
Bunky, his whole head covered in flea
shampoo foam. 'We shouldn't have
done the advert without you.'

'Yeah, I don't know what came over us,' said Nancy, rubbing flea shampoo into her armpits. 'Pleeeaaassseee forgive us!' she groaned, staggering towards me with her arms stretched out like some kind of foam monster.

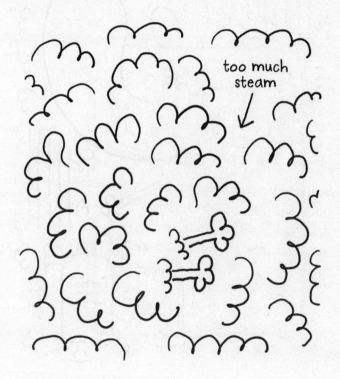

'Yuck, I'm gonna be sick from all this niceness,' said Darren, and I looked at the three of them covered in flea shampoo and smiled, thinking how it would be keel if we were all in a Feeko's Flea Shampoo advert one day.

'What a LUVVERLY day!' I beamed,
grabbing a handful of foam and
squodging it into Nancy's head.

'Isn't it glorious!' smiled Nancy, bonking
me on the nose.

'Feeko's Flea Shampoo for Dogs!' said
Bunky, picking up a handful of dead
fleas and doing his best advert smile.

I put my arms round him and Nancy, and Darren too, because I was in a good mood all of a sudden.

'It's the keelest!' we all shouted, but we didn't jump in the air and do a little dance, because that's extremely dangerous when you're in or around water. Plus I didn't want my pants to fall down.

The endy-poos.

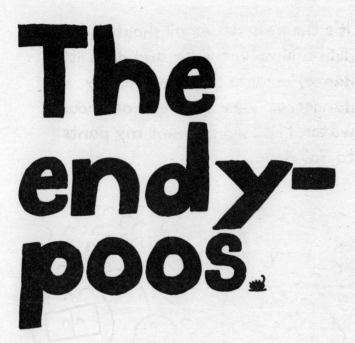

Draw some bugs

That is an order.

LOSERFACT

Jim Smith had nits about three times when he was a kid. One time when he had them and was looking in the mirror, he saw one carrying its dead friend along the top of his eyebrow.

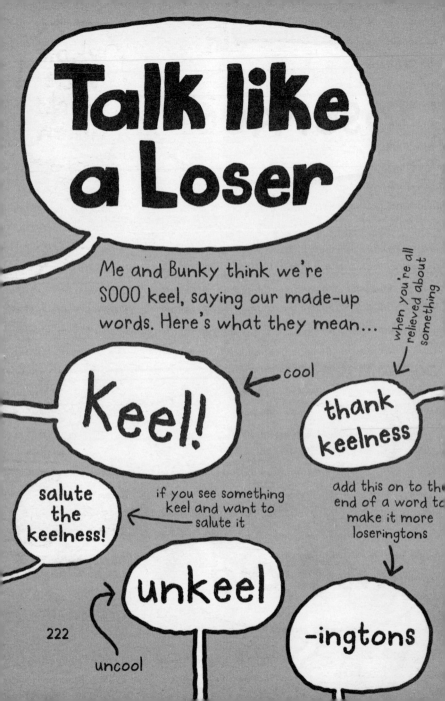

My 10 keelest questions EVER!

Here are the winners of my 'keel questions' competition. It was a competition where people sent in keel questions, and the top ten keelest ones got printed in this book, on page 224, which is this page. Enjoykeels!

person asking me a question

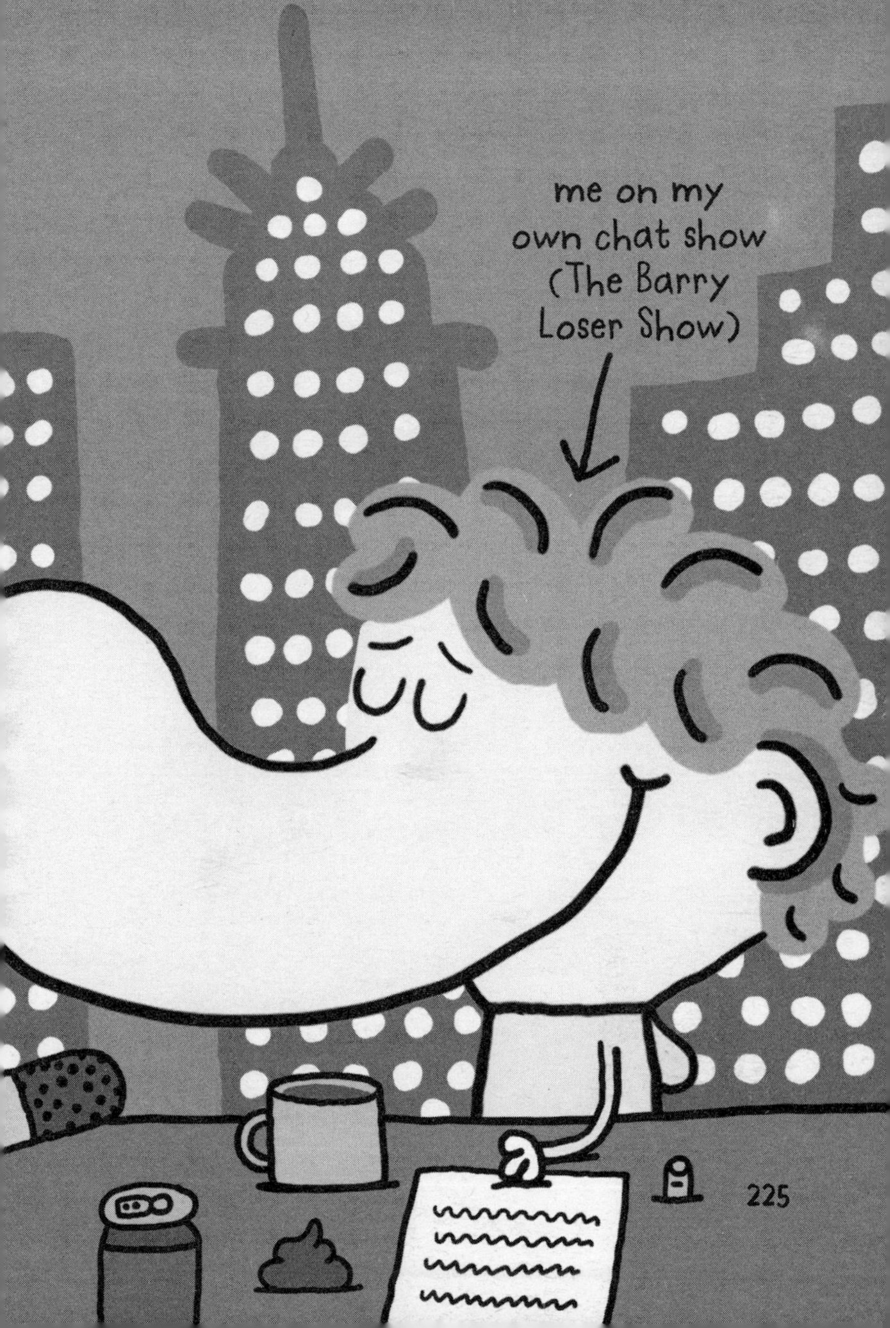
me on my own chat show (The Barry Loser Show)

GABE: Dear Barry, whatever happened to snailypoos?

Good morning Gabe, good question. Snailypoos is still alive, and now has nine hundred and seventy three children. We met up for a can of Fronkle just the other day, and apart from how tired he looks these days, he's just the same.

JACOB: Dear Jim, can you ask Barry what the hardest nose bonk he'd ever received was?

Good evening Jacob, I've just been on the phone to Barry and he says the hardest nose bonk he's ever received was from Anton Mildew's invisible friend Invis. Barry didn't even know it'd happened until Anton told him. That's why it was so hard - because it didn't even make sense. I mean, how can an invisible friend bonk your nose? (When I say hard, I mean hard to work out, by the way).

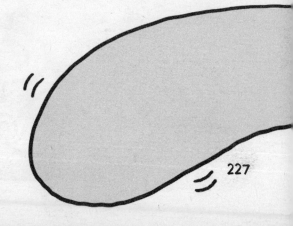

AISHA: Dear Jim, what shoe size is Barry Loser?

Hi Aisha, shoe sizes are different in Mogden - all shoes come in Keel, Keeler and Keelest. Barry's shoe size is Keelest.

ETHAN: Hi Barry, why is FUTURE RATBOY called FUTURE RATBOY?

Ethan, this is explained in my book, 'Future Ratboy and the Attack of the Killer Robot Grannies'. But you'll have to read the whole thing to understand. And even then you might not understand. But only if you can't speak English, because it's really not that difficult to understand.

HAZEL: Hi Jim, are your books for a special purpose or do you just like making them?

Hi Hazel, I've always liked making books. In fact, I have a box of little books I made all for myself, that hardly anyone else apart from me ever sees.

LILY AMBER: Dear Jim, what is the most embarrassing thing that's ever happened to you?

Hi Lily Amber, I once pooed myself at the beach in Lee Bay, North Devon when I was a kid. I was in my swimming trunks and had to walk back to the hotel room with my bum up against the wall the whole way so no one would notice. Beaches always used to make me need a poo. And libraries. I've told you the exact spot it happened in so you can visit it and imagine the scene better.

Jim

MORGAN: Dear Barry, when did you do your biggest blowoff and why?

Morgan, this is a very important question. My biggest ever blowoff was when me and Bunky were running away from Mrs Trumpet Face's house after we'd knocked on her door once. I'd been saving up the blowoff for three years, and now was the perfect time to use it! Its turbo powers helped me escape down an alleyway at superkeelness speed. Unfortunately the blowoff blew straight into Bunky's face and he fainted and was captured by the evil Mrs Trumpet Face, then taken back to her dungeon where he still is now. I just made that all up by the way.

ZUNAIR: Dear Jim, how do you get these mind-blowing ideas?

Hi Zunair, I like your name. It's like you're an aeroplane company. The answer to your question is in your question - I 'get' them - I don't look for them, they just pop up and I take them. Although you have to know when they've popped up I spose. I think mostly it's just that I'm really bored most of the time, so I try to entertain myself with whatever's going on inside my brain.

ARCHIE: Dear Barry, what's your favourite part about Not Bird?

Hi Archie, my favourite part about Not Bird is the little washing-instructions tag that sticks out of his bum. I'm talking about my cuddly Not Bird, of course. Although the real Not Bird also has a washing-instructions tag. I wish I had one of those sticking out of my bum, then I'd know what what temperature to wash myself at.

keel!

DANIEL: Hi Barry! Will you ever marry Nancy Verkenwerken?

Hi Daniel, who knowkeels! Maybe we could get married in one of my books, and have Bunky as our baby. Did you know that Nancy Verkenwerken is actually based on Jim Smith's childhood pen-friend Nancy Vankeerbergen?

Not Not Bird

These are some of the early designs for Not Bird:

colour them in!

and here's how he ended up looking

Come up with some
more Not Not Birds.
Maybe use these
shapes for them.

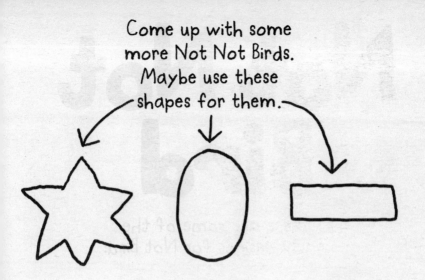

Draw them
here!

Guess the nose!

Whose noses are these noses?

A_____

B_____

C_____

D_____

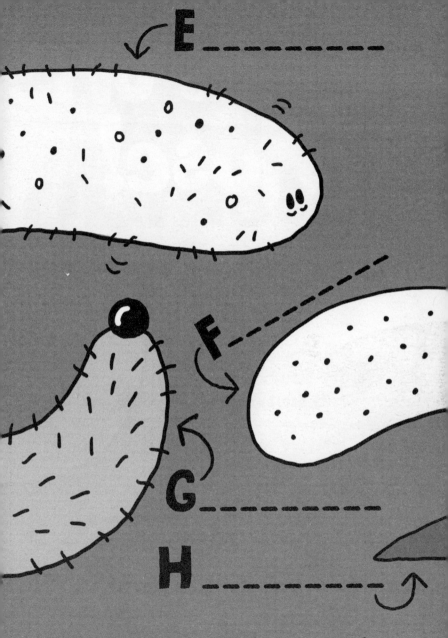

E_____
F
G_____
H_____

A Barry Loser B Bunky C Gordon Smugly D Darren Darrenofski
E Benjamin Bottle F Gaspar Pink G Future Ratboy H Not Bird

The loserfan quiz!

How much of a Barry Loser fan are you? Find out by answering these ridikeelous questions.

A. Who do Barry and Bunky call 'Cupboard Eyes'?

_ _ _ _ _ _ _ _

B. Whose china pig did Barry smash into ten pieces in his purple book, 'The Case of the Crumpled Carton'?

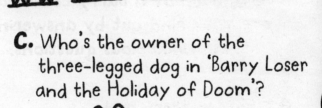

_ _ _ _ _ _ _ _

C. Who's the owner of the three-legged dog in 'Barry Loser and the Holiday of Doom'?

_ _ _ _ _ _

D. What does Barry say
instead of 'KEEL' in his
red book, 'I am STILL
not a Loser'?

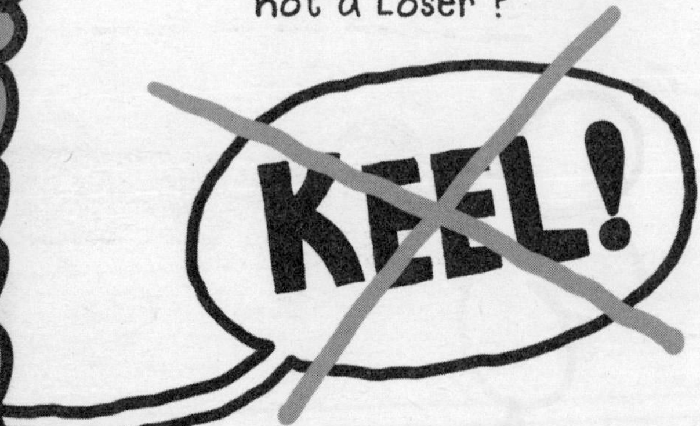

~~KEEL!~~

E. Who gets a fish finger
stuck on their forehead
in the blue book, 'I am
NOT a Loser'?

F. Whose Whatever Box
contained a worm
bracelet?

_ _ _ _ _ _ _ _ _ _

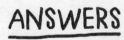

G. Who lived in a
house like this?

_ _ _ _ _ _ _ _

Design a superhero

Future Ratboy got zapped by lightning while he was inside a bin with his cuddly toy bird, Bird, an old TV set, and a rat.

That's how he ended up millions of years in the future as a half rat, half boy, half TV, with a cuddly flying bird as his sidekick.

Use this page to come up
with your own superhero -
make sure you know how
they got their superpowers,
and give them a sidekick!

You know how I
keep going on about
Future Ratboy the
whole time? Well
here are a few
pages from the new
Future Ratboy book,
FUTURE RATBOY AND THE
ATTACK OF THE KILLER
ROBOT GRANNIES!

DISASTER STRIKES

'COLIN SWEETIE, COME BACK HERE!'
shouted my mum, as I stretched the
scuba mask over my head and zoomed
out of the front door, past my dad
who was coming back in, minus the TV.

'I'VE GOT TO SAVE THE TELLY!' I shouted.
'OTHERWISE I'LL NEVER SEE ATTACK OF
THE KILLER ROBOT GRANNIES!'

A bolt of lightning hit the little apple tree in our front garden and a branch exploded, spraying tiny little bits of bark through the air.

'WAAAAAHHH! BE CAREFUL, MY DARLING!' screamed my mum, as I lifted the lid of our green plastic wheelie bin and dived into it, which is another thing I've always wanted to do.

KERFLUMP!

27

'Phew, that was close!' I whispered,
giving Bird a stroke and patting the TV.
My eyes were getting used to the pitch
blackness, and I noticed I was
sitting on a half-filled-up bin bag,
which was actually quite comfy.

'Squeak!' squeaked something, and
seeing as it couldn't have been Bird,
because he was just a cuddly toy bird
that couldn't speak, I looked around
the bin for something else that might
have made the noise. AND THAT WAS
WHEN I SPOTTED THE RAT.

'RAAAAAT!' I screamed.
Not that anyone
could hear me,
what with the
lightning bolt
hitting the bin.

MILLIONS OF YEARS LATER

I woke up and didn't know where I was. Then I remembered I was in a bin.

I lifted the lid and jumped out. It was morning and the little apple tree in my front garden was now a gigantic, ancient one. 'Coooool!' I said, and I looked up at my house, which was two times taller and more metal-looking than I remembered. 'Also coooool!' I smiled. I like saying 'cool', in case you haven't noticed.

'Mu-um! I'm ho-ome!' I shouted, knocking on the front door.

The door whooshed open like one of the ones at my local supermarket, and an old lady with a shiny metal head and red traffic-light eyes peered down at me. 'HELLO DEAR,' she bleeped, in a robotic voice.

MAVIS 3000

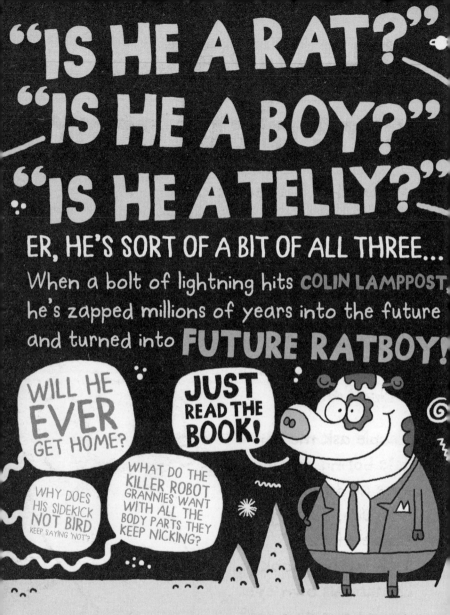

About the eye dotterer

Jim Smith is the keelest kids' book eye dotterer in the whole world amen. He graduated from art school with first class honours (the best you can get) and went on to create the branding for a sweet little chain of coffee shops. He also designs cards and gifts under the name Waldo Pancake.

'People ask me if it gets boring dotting eyes all day long,' says Jim, dotting a couple of eyes without even looking. Because his own eyes don't have any dots at all.

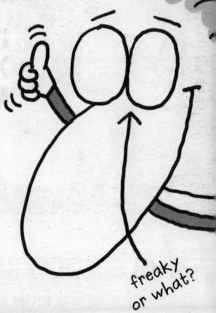

freaky or what?

Check out my other keel books!

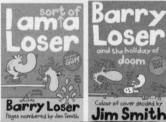

Miss Spivak

Fay Snoggles

Mr Whatsitoo

Gino

Gino

Donut Beard

Mr Koops

Future Ratboy

Not Bird

Trev or Trevor